In

Dona Herweck Rice

Publishing Credits

Rachelle Cracchiolo, M.S.Ed., *Publisher*
Conni Medina, M.A.Ed., *Managing Editor*
Nika Fabienke, Ed.D., *Content Director*
Véronique Bos, *Creative Director*
Shaun N. Bernadou, *Art Director*
Carol Huey-Gatewood, M.A.Ed., *Editor*
Valerie Morales, *Associate Editor*
Courtney Roberson, *Senior Graphic Designer*

Image Credits: All images from iStock and/or Shutterstock.

Teacher Created Materials
5301 Oceanus Drive
Huntington Beach, CA 92649-1030
www.tcmpub.com

ISBN 978-1-4938-9825-1

Printed in Malaysia. Thumbprints.24790

They are in  .

school

They are in  .

traffic

They are in 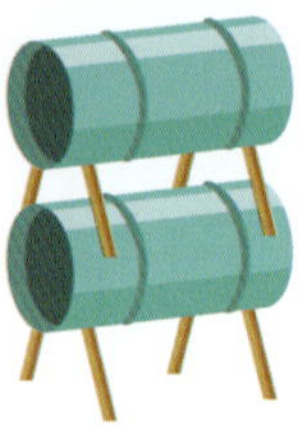 .

tunnels

They are in  .

forts

They are in  .

swimsuits

They are in  .

raincoats

They are in  .

bubbles

They are in  .

pajamas

They are in  .

blankets

They are in 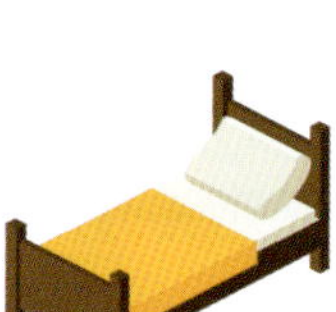 .

bed

High-Frequency Words

are

in

they